Stefan's Secret Fear

Donna Reid Vann
Illustrated by John Haysom

A LION PICTURE STORY
Oxford · Batavia · Sydney

Everyone who lived in the German town of Twist, on the River Rhine, thought Stefan was the bravest boy around. He would climb to the tip-top of the tallest tree, to capture a nervous cat. He had once flung himself fully clothed into the river, to rescue Dorie Dinkel's doll. Stefan was quick to agree that he had plenty of pluck.

"I would even go into the Haunted House at night," he often boasted, "all by myself."

Brave though he was, Stefan had a secret, which he dearly hoped no one in Twist ever discovered. In spite of his daring deeds, there was a deep-down part of him that was afraid, though he could not have said exactly of what. He felt it at night, as he lay in his bedroom overlooking the water, watching reflections flicker on the dark ceiling. His fears would come creeping into the room, wearing awful shapes: dragons and wild beasts, giants and wicked gnomes. Stefan lay shivering, his courage gone, as the fantastic figures danced around his bed.

"Go away!" he shouted as loud as he could without waking his parents. But the monsters merely grinned and whirled all the more merrily.

Captain Lang, who piloted the ferry boat every hour from Twist across to the opposite shore, was Stefan's special friend. He was the one person who might have guessed Stefan's secret. Stefan admired the captain and was especially eager to convince him of his own courage.

"I guess I'm about the bravest boy around," said Stefan carelessly one afternoon, as he stood in his usual place at the captain's elbow.

"That so?" grinned the captain, as he nosed the ferry slightly upstream, to keep clear of a pleasure cruiser. Its gleaming white decks were crowded with people, all pointing cameras at the town's half-timbered houses and the ancient castle on the hill.

"Well, everybody says so," Stefan replied.

Captain Lang rubbed his mammoth moustache with one finger. "When I was young," he said, "I pretended I was totally fearless. No one ever guessed I was a coward inside."

Stefan was silent. He couldn't imagine the captain being afraid of anything. Did the captain suspect that he, Stefan, was really a scaredy-cat at heart? Stefan wished he could tell him about the monsters that came in the night.

By day Stefan could usually forget his fears in
the delight of living right over the rippling river.
Long barges churned downstream loaded to the
limit, their decks scarcely an inch above the water.
Gulls swooped and cawed, and swans glided
gracefully in the shallows. Stefan and his best
friend Marcus liked to pedal their bikes headlong
on the river path, racing the mighty cruisers. The
cruisers always won, but the captains would wave
at them, as if to say, "You did your best! Better
luck next time!"

One fine day in early spring Stefan and Marcus biked with their friends to the Haunted House. They stopped by the tumble-down gate to plan, as they often did, for the time when they would sneak inside. They would have done this long before, only some of them had second thoughts. Would there be ghosts?

"What are we waiting for?" Stefan asked. "I'm not scared — I'll even go in by myself, if you want."

Marcus stuck out his chin. "You say that every time," he complained, "but I don't see you doing it. Why don't you go in first? Then, if nothing happens to you, we'll follow."

Stefan trembled inwardly. He thought he caught a glimpse of a creature or two behind the broken windowpanes of the Haunted House. If he didn't go inside, the others would know he was only a scaredy-cat after all.

He took a deep breath and gave the rusty gate
a shove. Stefan stepped forward three small steps.
Fear caught in his throat; he could scarcely breathe.
The black door of the old house looked like an
open mouth, just waiting for him to walk in. What
would he find inside?

Stefan froze. He could not move another inch.

"What's the matter?" Marcus called out behind
him. "You scared?"

Stefan turned and stared Marcus right in the eye.

"Yes," he replied, "I'm scared."

He stalked over to his bike and wheeled off as
fast as he could towards the Rhine and his friend
the captain.

"Scaredy-cat!" Marcus shouted after him,
and some of the others giggled.

On the ferry boat Captain Lang let Stefan steer.
They rode silently for a moment, then Stefan
blurted, "I tried to go into the Haunted House
today, but I couldn't. I thought the creatures might
be there — the ones that come to me every night in
my room. Now all the kids know I'm a coward!"

"Well," said the captain, "remember I told you
that I was a coward, too. It's not the worst thing in
the world to be. Most people are scared of
something, even if they don't show it."

The sun was just beginning to dip behind the hills on the opposite bank, so the river was strewn with sparkling diamonds of light. Captain Lang did not seem to notice the one large tear trickling its way down Stefan's cheek.

"See that light?" the captain asked. "Wherever light goes, it chases away the darkness. Those fears are like darkness deep inside you; you need light to drive them away."

"It doesn't help to leave the lamp on in my room," said Stefan. "I've tried that and the creatures still come."

"I don't mean lamplight," said the captain, stroking his moustache thoughtfully. "I mean God's light. God *is* light – he is my light. If you have God with you, it's like having a good strong light shining out into the darkness. Then you don't need to be so afraid."

"How can God be with me?" Stefan asked, keeping his hands on the wheel and his eyes on the approaching bank.

"He's just waiting for us to ask him," said the captain. "If I were you, I'd talk to him about it. That's what I do. You can talk to him anytime, you know, about anything."

This was the season when the mountain snows begin to melt. The snow had been late and heavy that year, and the spring sun sent it rushing pell-mell down into swollen streams and rivers. Not many days after Stefan's talk with the captain, word reached the town of Twist: flood waters were coming! The excitement of the flood drove everything else out of Stefan's mind.

Every grown-up and child had to help prepare for the flood. River folk were used to it: they bought enough food for a week and hauled all their belongings upstairs. Most people lived on an upper level to begin with, since the ground floor was bound to be flooded every year or two.

Stefan helped his father carry tools from the garage and parked his bicycle upstairs in the front hall. They left the rubber dinghy downstairs, but tied it securely to the wall so that it wouldn't float away. There was no school, and Marcus was allowed to stay with Stefan until the waters went down. The boys were full of plans for their school-free days.

Early next morning, when Stefan pushed back his bedroom shutters, he could scarcely see the far shore of the Rhine. The sky pressed down heavily like the underside of a grey metal pot. The brown surface of the water looked flat and shallow as cardboard, yet it moved swiftly. No boats were allowed during floodtime, so the darkened river was empty.

Stefan ran downstairs, and saw that the water was already coming in the open garage door. He was about to call Marcus to come and see when he heard a cry booming loudly over the river:

"Help! Help!"

Stefan waded to the door and peered out. He could just make out a small something shooting downstream at a terrible speed.

Again the cry came: "Help!"

A man was in the water!

Hardly knowing what he did, Stefan untied the dinghy, pushed it through the doorway and jumped in. At once the river grabbed hold and wrenched the tiny boat forward into its rushing flow. The man was bobbing far ahead and Stefan spun after him, clutching the dinghy's ropes as the water sucked him greedily onward.

The river was no longer friendly; it had become an evil, dark thing which had the power to destroy. Neither he nor the man in the water could do anything to save themselves. Stefan squinted his eyes to see more clearly, but the man seemed to have disappeared. Fear began to rise like a darkness within him.

Suddenly he thought of Captain Lang's words: *light chases away darkness*.

If God were here with me, he thought, his light could drive away my fears. But how can I get him to come?

Then he remembered what the captain had said. He could talk to God! Stefan had never done that before, but he decided to try.

"Dear God," he whispered softly, hardly hearing his words as the wind whisked them away. "The captain says I can talk to you, and that you'll come to me with your light. I need you to come right now, God. Everything seems so dark and I'm scared!"

There was a break in the lowering clouds and a patch of daylight peeked through. In spite of his fear, Stefan felt a flicker of hope. Just then he saw the man. He was tangled in the branches of a half-submerged willow up ahead, and Stefan was heading straight for him.

"Hallo!" Stefan shouted. "Grab on, if you can!"

In the nick of time the man caught sight of Stefan and reached out. Stefan grasped the man's hand and held on with all his might, for the river wanted to snatch him away. The man managed to make the dinghy's rope fast to the willow and heaved himself on board.

Stefan was astonished to see the dripping moustache and beaming face of his friend, the captain!

The two huddled together in the dinghy, waiting for someone to see them and send the flood patrol boat.

"I fell in when I went down to check the ferry's moorings," said the captain. "You did a crazy thing, but it saved my life. Thank you for being brave enough to come after me."

"I was really scared to death," Stefan admitted. "But then I told God I wanted him to be with me. And I'm sure he heard, because my fear didn't matter so much any more. That's when I saw you."

Captain Lang grinned and patted Stefan's shoulder.

"There's the boat!" the captain exclaimed, as he fished out a soggy handkerchief to wave.

"Do you really think God can chase my fear-monsters away?" Stefan asked as the patrol boat churned towards them.

"You'll never get rid of fear completely," said the captain. "But as for those monsters, why don't you give it a try?"

Back at Stefan's house, his mother cried a few tears of relief and his father told him he was proud. Marcus called him a hero.

"I take it all back about you being a scaredy-cat," he said. "Anyway, I'm afraid of the Haunted House myself."

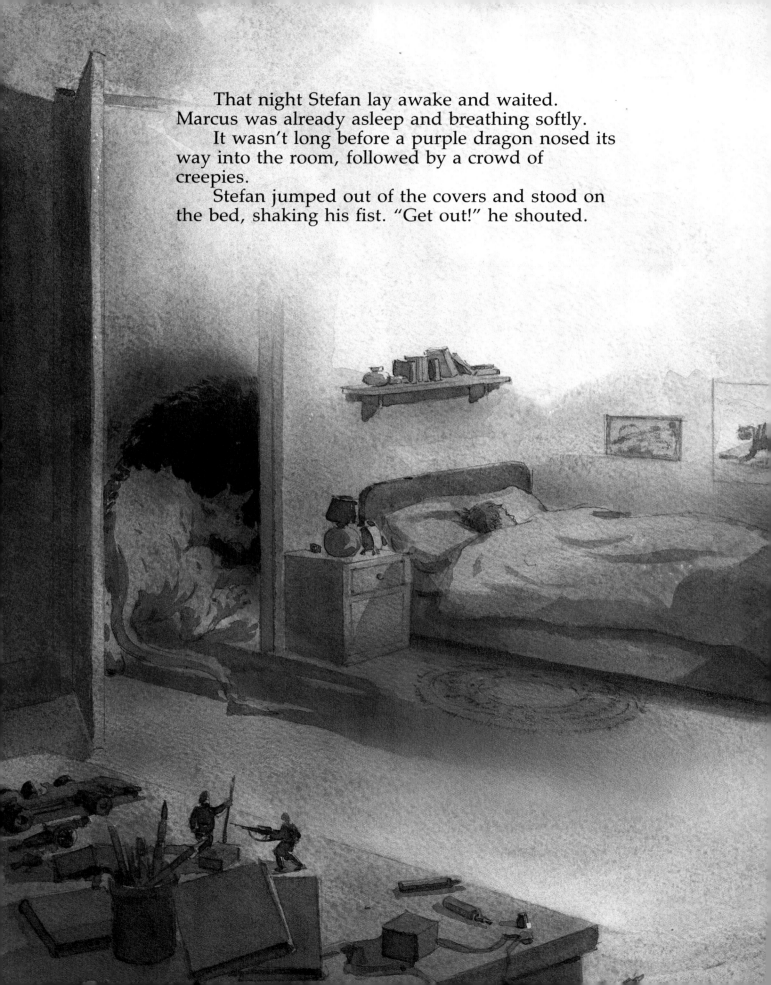

That night Stefan lay awake and waited.
Marcus was already asleep and breathing softly.
It wasn't long before a purple dragon nosed its
way into the room, followed by a crowd of
creepies.
Stefan jumped out of the covers and stood on
the bed, shaking his fist. "Get out!" he shouted.

"God is with me now. His light is stronger than darkness — all you dark things have to go!"

The creatures vanished.

A moment later Marcus sat up sleepily.

"Who were you yelling at?" he mumbled.

"No one," Stefan replied as he smiled and snuggled down into his pillow. "No one at all."

AFTERWORD

Stefan thought he was the only
person with secret fears. But he
learned that the captain, and his
friend Marcus, were also sometimes
afraid. Every one of us is afraid of
something. But sometimes being
afraid makes us do silly things, or
stops us doing something we really
want to do.

Stefan found that he could talk
about his fear with a trusted friend.
A big fear seems smaller when a
friend understands.

The most important thing Stefan
learned was that, with God, he had
the courage to face his fears. Stefan
will be afraid many times in his life,
and he will have to remember that
God is still with him. We may never
get rid of all our fears. Yet when
God is with us, we have someone
who is much greater than any fear,
and who can take care of us even
when we are afraid.

There is no actual town of Twist on
the River Rhine in Germany. But
there are many towns just like the
one in which Stefan lived, which are
flooded when the river is high.